D1575923

Weekly Reader Children's Book Club presents
Fourth of July Raid

Other Books by Wilma Pitchford Hays

CHRISTMAS ON THE MAYFLOWER
PILGRIM THANKSGIVING
THE STORY OF VALENTINE
FREEDOM

Fourth of July Raid

by Wilma Pitchford Hays

Illustrated by Peter Burchard

Xerox Education Publications

"We Therefore Solemnly Publish and Declare that these United Colonies are Free and Independent States...and for the Support of this Declaration, we Mutually Pledge to each other our Lives, our Fortunes and our Sacred Honor."

© 1959 by Wilma Pitchford Hays

Illustrations used by arrangement with Peter Burchard.

COVER ART BY RAYMOND KEANE

Publishing, Executive and Editorial Offices:
Xerox Education Publications
Middletown, Connecticut 06457

Printed in U.S.A. All rights reserved. This book may not be reproduced in whole or in part in any form or format without permission in writing from the publisher.

Library of Congress Catalog Card Number: 59-5234

Xerox® is a trademark of Xerox Corporation.

Weekly Reader Children's Book Club edition

To my niece and nephews—Kathy, Gary, Fred, Johnny, Phil, Matt and two Bills.

Tom Morris sat at the kitchen table in the Morris mansion house and helped his cousin, Elizabeth, shell peas for tomorrow's Fourth of July dinner. The long table was loaded with roasts of mutton and pork and chickens. Tom sniffed the odors of spicy pudding and fresh baked bread.

"Mother must have invited a hundred people," he said. "There's enough food to feed an army."

A frightened look came into Elizabeth's blue eyes. "Tom," she asked, "do you think it's true that British warships were sighted not far from New Haven harbor?"

"British warships have sailed up and down Long Island Sound all summer," Tom said. "But the British know there is no army here to attack."

"Of course there *was* an army in Philadelphia," Elizabeth said. "Just the same, I'll be glad when your father and John come back from scouting the shore—and tell us the warships aren't coming here."

Tom looked at her bent head, with hair as dark red as his own. He was tired of hearing Elizabeth tell how bravely the men of Philadelphia had fought when the British captured that city where Elizabeth lived.

"Don't be scared," he said. "The men of New Haven town are just as brave as the men of Philadelphia."

Elizabeth ran her thumb down a pod to push out the peas.

"I guess I'm just excited," she said. "I can hardly wait for midnight when the bonfires will be lighted all along the harbor shore—and the cannon will fire from Black Rock Fort and on Beacon Hill."

Tom felt a shiver of excitement move down his back. "It will seem strange for the cannon on Beacon Hill to sound without meaning an alarm," he said.

Every Sunday since the War for Independence

began, Tom had sat in the Morris pew in the Stone Meeting House and heard the minister read the official warning before the service:

"The signal for a British attack shall be three shots from the cannon on Beacon Hill. Every Patriot shall immediately provide himself with musket and a full supply of cartridges and proceed to his assigned post to defend his home and his country."

Elizabeth stripped the peas from the last pod and stood up to pour them from her bowl into an iron kettle. The rattle of the peas woke a small pig who was asleep on a braided rug in front of the fireplace. The pig grunted and opened one eye.

"Curly-tail," Tom said, "what would Father say if he found you in the house again?"

Elizabeth lifted the pet pig from the rug. "He's spoiled," she said, and stroked the pig's sleepy head. "I put him in the pigpen a dozen times today. Every time he rooted under the fence and ran back into the house."

"I'll take him," Tom said and he tucked the pig under his arm.

Curly-tail *was* spoiled. He had been born a runt and was brought to the house. He lived in a box by the fireplace until he grew strong. He still thought he belonged with the family.

Curly-tail squealed and tried to wriggle free as Tom left the kitchen and walked into the dark barnyard. He reached the fence and dropped the small pig over.

"Father had a new hoghouse built," he said. "Now be good and live there where you belong."

Tom turned back. How pleasant his home looked with its many windows lighted. In an upstairs bedroom he could see his mother putting his younger brothers and sisters to bed. He looked beyond the house toward the cove. Soon his father and his older brother, John, would be coming back from their nightly patrol of the harbor shore. It was too dark to see across the salt grass meadow to the water.

Tom had almost reached the kitchen door,

when he heard the boom of a cannon. He stopped and listened. The cannon boomed again. And again.

The kitchen door flew open and Elizabeth stood in the lighted doorway.

"Tom," she cried, "Wasn't that Beacon Cannon? It's much too early to begin celebrating."

"Maybe someone couldn't wait until midnight," Tom said.

Elizabeth stepped into the night beside him. "It *was* the Beacon, Tom. And it fired three times. That's the warning!"

Tom heard the tremble in her voice.

"I told you not to be afraid," he said. "You're safe now staying with us."

"When I was so frightened in Philadelphia," Elizabeth almost whispered, "Father told me to remember how brave the men were who signed the Declaration of Independence for us. They knew their homes might be burned. They knew they might be killed if the British captured them. But every man signed."

Tom thought he heard something in the darkness and wished his father were home.

"The men risked their lives," Elizabeth went on, "and their fortunes and their sacred honor— for liberty—just as the declaration says. . . . Tom, do you think we can be that brave?"

Elizabeth was always saying things like that and it troubled Tom. Three years ago Elizabeth had crowded into the State House Yard with other people of Philadelphia. She had heard the Declaration of Independence read aloud for the very first time. And she never let anyone forget it.

Tom *hoped* he would be brave if the enemy came. But how could he be sure, when he hadn't even seen a Redcoat?

"Listen," he said. "Horses are galloping this way. It must be Father and John."

His father and brother reined their horses before the house and leaped to the ground.

"British warships are entering the harbor," his father said. "It looks like a real raid this time."

Tom and Elizabeth ran behind him into the

13

kitchen. Silently they watched him pull extra loads of cartridges from the gunrack on the wall.

"Elizabeth," Mr. Morris said, "go upstairs and get Mother. Be careful not to wake the children yet. Tell her John and I are joining the men at the shore. If we can't keep the British from landing, I'll come back and warn her. John is yoking the oxen to the cart, in case she has to escape with the children."

As Elizabeth ran up the stairs, Tom's father turned to him. "Son, you must help Mother. Hide every valuable you can carry. Hide them away from the house, in the woods, and ditches and salt grass. If the British burn our home, we'll have something left."

Tom watched his father gallop away. He turned back and stood in the middle of the kitchen, not knowing what to hide first. Surely no one would set fire to his home. But his mother and Elizabeth must believe it could happen. They were hurrying down the stairs, holding up their full long skirts to keep from tripping. His mother gave instructions as she ran.

"We must hide our clothing and bedding, the

china and silver, and the big box with the family Bible and important papers," she said.

"We'll have to work fast," Tom said. "I hear firing already."

The three of them rushed in and out of the house with their arms full. They tucked quilts under low leafy bushes which grew in the ditches beside the road. They carried the china dishes into the salt meadow and laid them in the high coarse grass. By lantern light Tom dug a hole in the potato patch and buried the silver.

"Make it look as if we've been digging new potatoes," Elizabeth said. "That's the way we did in Philadelphia."

They worked for hours. When his mother ran into the parlor, it seemed to Tom that there couldn't be anything left to hide except the furniture, which was too heavy.

"My beautiful curtains," his mother said. "I worked months to spin the yarn for these and dye it and weave the cloth. I won't have the Redcoats burn my curtains—or steal them to hang in a British home."

Tom helped her pull the curtains from the windows and roll and tie them in a pack.

"Tom, do hide them in a safe, dry place," his mother begged. "But hurry, the firing seems heavier. We may have to leave any time. Elizabeth and I must stay here and wake the children."

She helped Tom lift the pack of curtains onto his back. He bent forward under their weight. This pack was too large to hide in bushes or grass. He must carry it into the woods and he must go alone.

Tom made his way through the moonlight to the stone wall behind the house. He moved along it, past the barnyard, and into the deep woods. Under the shadows of the trees, it was very dark. What if Redcoats had landed and were already waiting here?

The Morris house was the first on the east side of New Haven harbor. Below it, where Long Island Sound joined the harbor, was a lonely point where the enemy could have landed unseen.

The heavy pack of curtains shifted on Tom's back. Perhaps he had gone far enough. He could cover the pack with leaves. But his mother had cautioned him to find a safe, dry place.

Then he remembered a little cave he and Elizabeth had found one day. He pushed through the darkness under the trees until he came to the cave. Honeysuckle and bittersweet grew over the opening, so that no one would know there was an entrance. Tom lifted the curtain of vines and stared at the inky blackness under the rock. He felt his heart beat like a great drum against his ribs. He thrust the curtains under the rock and ran all the way back to the house.

For a moment he rested against the kitchen door to catch his breath. Morning light was coming into the sky. The boom of heavy guns told him that British warships were already in New Haven harbor below his home.

In the kitchen Tom found his father helping his mother and Elizabeth dress sleepy little brothers and sisters.

"We couldn't stop them," his father was saying. "Half the Redcoats landed across the harbor to take New Haven town—and half landed below our house on the Point. Thousands of British are marching this way along the shore."

Tom felt his face grow as bloodless as his mother's and Elizabeth's. The Redcoats were really coming.

"John is bringing the oxcart now," his father said. "Mother, you drive up the cartway as far north as you can into the valley. I must stay and fight with the men to hold the enemy."

"We'll need food." Tom's mother hurried to the table where the good things for the Fourth of July feast were ready.

Tom helped her wrap cloth around loaves of bread and puddings and roasts, and place them in willow baskets. Even the little children were given food to carry. Still much food was left.

Tom heard the heavy-footed oxen draw the cart to a stop outside the kitchen door and snort when the heavy gunfire sounded.

Mr. Morris lifted the children into the great oxcart. "Everyone goes but Tom," he said. "I'll need you, Son. We're going to save this house if we can."

"Let me help," Elizabeth cried from the back of the cart.

Her uncle shook his head and urged the oxen forward.

Tom heard wild squealing from the pigpen. Frightened by the boom of guns, the pigs broke their fence. They rushed away into the fields of tall ripe rye, all except one small pig. Curly-tail raced for Tom. He raised his pink snout and squealed. Tom caught up the pig and ran after the oxcart.

"Take Curly-tail," he cried. "I don't want the Redcoats to have him for their dinner."

Elizabeth leaned over the end of the cart and took the pet pig.

"Hurry, Tom," his father called and Tom followed him into the house. "I've sent the hired men to run the sheep and cattle and horses into

the woods," Mr. Morris said. "You and I are going to set out a feast for these British officers that will make their eyes bulge."

Tom stopped in the middle of the family room and stared at his father. A feast for the officers who would burn their home and maybe even kill them or take them prisoners!

His father was pulling the long table away from the wall and Tom took an end to help.

"You don't really mean to feed them, do you, Father?"

"Ours is the first house the Redcoats will reach," his father said. "It's a long time since they've seen food as good as this. Maybe our Independence feast will keep them busy until our neighbors can escape—and maybe the officers will enjoy it so much that they won't burn our home."

Tom ran and lifted a roast onto a pewter platter and placed it in the center of the long table. A bit of the meat broke off and he popped it into his mouth. He was hungry, but he mustn't think of himself now.

He and his father loaded the table with roasts

and bread, with bowls of red-ware pottery filled with fruit, with baked puddings in ironware pots. His father brought jugs of wine from the cellar. Tom fetched the cone of precious white sugar in its wooden bucket. He brought chunks of salt and the salt breaker. If these British could be stopped, it was worth offering the family's best.

Enemy firing was so close now that Tom ran to the window. A company of Redcoats was within a stone's throw of the house.

"Run, Tom," his father called.

Together they raced out the front door, reached the stone wall and crept along it to the gate. They dashed for the woods. Bullets whistled over their heads as they reached the trees.

"Tom," his father said, "I must get back to that fighting. You follow the cartway north and try to overtake your mother."

"Can't I go with you? Tom pleaded.

"You're too young for fighting," his father said. "And you could be taken prisoner and chained in the dungeon of a filthy prison ship."

Tom shivered. "I could stop at Black Rock Fort," he said, "and help the men there."

His father shook his head. "We have nineteen men at the fort and three cannon—against thousands of Redcoats. It can't hold long."

Tom's heart sank. At the fort were his friends and neighbors, the Tuttles, the Pardees and the Chidseys.

"Hurry to the cartway and head north," his father said again and disappeared into the woods.

Tom ran to the narrow cartway which led through woods and past homes along the shore of New Haven harbor. He followed the winding turns.

When the rough road dipped through a peat bog, he lost one of his shoes in the muck. He bent to pick it up and heard the shuffle of feet. The sound came from behind the stone wall which separated the cartway from the deep woods.

Was it a Redcoat? Tom was afraid to move even to put on his shoe. He saw the barrel of a musket come up over the wall.

"Tom Morris, it's you," an astonished voice cried.

Tom ran to the wall and faced his neighbors, Joseph Tuttle and his son, Josiah.

"Has the fort fallen?" he asked.

"The British were on us from all sides," Josiah said. "We spiked our cannon so the guns would be no good to the Redcoats. Then we escaped."

"We're going to make another stand on Beacon Hill," Mr. Tuttle said. "First we must warn the family to escape."

"I can warn them," Tom said.

"Hurry, then," Mr. Tuttle said. "The Redcoats are close behind us."

Tom ran back along the cartway until he came to the Tuttle rye field. He cut through the ripe grain to the orchard, reached the house and knocked on the door. Mrs. Tuttle opened it, her small children clustered behind her.

"Mr. Tuttle says you must run," Tom said. "The British are marching this way along the cartway."

"Quickly, children, into the rye fields," Mrs. Tuttle cried. "Crouch down and say your prayers."

"That ripe rye would burn like powder," Tom said. "The woods are safer."

Mrs. Tuttle carried the baby. Tom took the hands of two of the youngest and they ran into the woods. Suddenly Mrs. Tuttle clapped her hand to her mouth.

"I must go back," she said. "I forgot my husband's papers."

"You can't," Tom said. "The British may be there now."

"I promised Joseph to keep our papers with me," she said. "They are important records and the deeds to our home."

Tom knew she mustn't go back to the house with the small children who couldn't run fast.

"You keep the children safe," he said. "I'll go back for your papers."

"On the cherry table by the door," Mrs. Tuttle called. "I laid them there when you knocked."

Tom had gone only a little way when he heard

shots close by. He felt his courage slipping. What if the British had already reached the Tuttle house? He had promised and he must try. Quickly, before he could change his mind, he ran through the trees to the orchard.

He peered from behind an apple tree. The house seemed empty. He dashed to the door, found the papers inside and tucked them into his blouse. As he turned to leave, he saw the Redcoats swarming through the orchard. He dodged behind the door.

Tom thought of what his father had said—the dungeon of a prison ship was filthy and the chains were heavy. He could scarcely breathe as he tried to flatten himself against the wall.

He heard a Brittish officer shout, "Halt," and the sound of marching feet stopped. Tom peeked through the crack at the back of the half-open door and his heart jumped.

British soldiers were drawn up in front of the house. Facing them were Mr. Tuttle and Josiah, their hands tied behind their backs. British muskets were leveled at them and British swords were at their backs.

Trembling, Tom tried to think of some way to help his friends. He looked around for something to throw. If he could startle the British, the Tuttles might have a chance to run. Then he realized that his friends could be killed if they moved. He could only wait and hope the Redcoats didn't capture him, too.

The British officer in charge was talking to a man in civilian clothes. Tom knew the man. He was a Tory, a British sympathizer from New Haven town, who had been a friend of Tom's family and the Tuttles before the war.

Now the officer turned to the Tuttles.

"Rebels," he said. "This loyal British subject has asked me to give you another chance. I will not burn your home and you may go free, *if* you will swear to lay down your arms and never take them up against Britain again."

Tom breathed more easily. Joseph and Josiah wouldn't be shot. They had only to promise that they wouldn't fight again with the Patriots.

Mr. Tuttle looked at his son, and the boy shook his head. The father answered the officer clearly.

"I will not promise to lay down my arms, not for all the gold in the British kingdom."

The Tory from New Haven town spoke angrily. "Don't forget, Joseph Tuttle, you and I are Englishmen, too."

"And don't you forget," Mr. Tuttle answered, "that Englishmen have always fought for their rights—even against their own unjust kings."

The Redcoats grumbled. One shouted, "Run the rebel through."

As several stepped forward with swords lifted, Tom almost cried out. He pressed his sleeve against his mouth so that he wouldn't give himself away.

"You cannot kill us," Mr. Tuttle said. "We demand the rights of prisoners of war."

The officer waved his sword. "I've offered to save your lives and your home," he said. "What are you fighting for, anyway?"

"For God and my freeman's rights," Mr. Tuttle answered.

"You'll get your rights in the old hulk *Jersey*," the officer cried.

Tom shivered. The *Jersey* was the most dreaded of all prison ships. He blinked rapidly as he saw the soldier turn his friends and prod them toward the cartway with the points of their swords.

His sympathy was mixed with pride in their courage. Joseph and Josiah must be afraid yet they didn't give up fighting for freedom—not even to save their home and themselves.

From his hiding place behind the door, Tom saw two Redcoats were coming with flaming torches toward the house and rye field. One of them stopped outside the door. Tom's heart beat so hard he felt the soldier would surely hear it. A moment later he smelled smoke and heard the crackle of flames as the house began to burn.

Choking, Tom almost ran out the door into the soldier's arms. Just in time he remembered the dungeon of the old hulk, *Jersey*.

He raced through the house, broke a kitchen

window and jumped into the garden. He landed in the soft earth, his feet braced apart. Which way should he go?

He couldn't escape through the blazing rye field. If he ran for the woods, the British might see him and shoot. He lay down between two rows of fat cabbages.

The heat of the burning house grew hotter and hotter until he had to crawl between the rows to the edge of the garden. At last he reached a tree and pulled himself up behind it.

He could no longer see a Redcoat anywhere, but the sound of fighting was all around him. He slipped through the woods until he came to a narrow salt grass meadow between New Haven harbor and the cartway. What he saw down in the harbor brought him to a halt.

On his left the harbor was filled with warships blasting the shore with cannon ball. On his right, the cartway was filled with fighting Patriots and Redcoats. The Patriots were backing step by step along the road, stopping every few paces to

fire their muskets on the rows of advancing enemy. Tom realized that there were thousands of Redcoats against only a few hundred Patriots.

He could see that the Patriots were trying to reach the earthworks on Beacon Hill just beyond the cartway. The field gun they were hauling in the rear bogged down in the road. Men strained to move it but couldn't.

"Run," Tom shouted. "Leave it. Don't let the Redcoats get you."

A cannon ball from the warships dug into the meadow in front of him. Another sheared off the top of the tree under which he was standing. He ducked. He couldn't stay here.

He looked toward Beacon Hill, where the Patriots were making another stand. The British had halted and were spread out like a great red sea at the foot of the hill, just out of reach of the fire from the Patriots' one big gun at the top.

Tom wished he could reach the hill. He had often played with the Tuttle and Pardee boys in the old Indian burial ground at the north end of

Beacon Hill. If he could reach that burying ground, he knew places where he could hide.

While Tom waited for a chance to race across the meadow, the sun grew so hot that he loosened his collar. Smoke choked him and he longed for a drink of water and something to eat.

He heard the firing grow heavier and saw that the Redcoats were storming the hill. Patriot fire sent them reeling back. The Redcoats stormed a second time.

This was Tom's chance. He sprinted across the meadow and crouched behind the stone wall. The roar of battle was so wild in his ears that he could hardly think but he knew he must get out of the line of fire.

He crept along the wall until he was beyond the fierce fighting and reached a huddle of frightened cows. The animals broke and ran across the cartway. Tom ran among them and gained the safety of the far side of the hill.

In the burial ground he rested in a wild plum thicket until he could catch his breath. Halfway up the end of the hill, he could see a rock ledge. He knew that a well-hidden Indian trail led to the ledge. If he could reach that ledge, he could hide under the rock and be safe from shots. But the climb was a long, hard one.

He looked toward the swamp which stretched a long way behind Beacon Hill. Thick pampas grass covered the swamp. The brown plumes and sharp green leaves were higher than a man's head. Tom remembered that pools of water lay between the hummocks.

At the thought of water, his throat ached and he knew he must have a drink.

He had gone only a little way into the rustly pampas grass when he came on a spring. He knelt beside it and splashed water onto his hot face before he lay on his stomach and drank deeply. The water tasted sweet and cool. He rested a little and drank again. He was so thirsty that even if he drank all day he wouldn't have enough.

Suddenly shots whistled over his head. He

heard the thunder of footsteps and the crashing sounds of men running through the tall pampas grass. Could they be Redcoats? He tried to flatten himself into the soft damp earth and hide. A foot struck his ankle and a man fell on his knees beside Tom. Tom turned his head, trembling, and found himself looking into the astonished face of a neighbor, young Mr. Pardee.

"Sh-h-h," Mr. Pardee said when Tom started to speak.

The crashing sounds were all around them as if a herd of cattle were stampeding. Two more Patriots dropped down beside Tom, then another and another, until there were a dozen men in the little group beside the spring.

"Did we lose Beacon Hill?" Tom asked when the firing died down.

"They were too much for us," Mr. Pardee said. "We had to spike the cannon and run."

"Just in time, too," another man said. "I could feel those Redcoats breathing on the back of my neck."

Tom swallowed. Black Rock Fort was lost and Beacon Hill, and with them, the Patriots' only big guns. The enemy outnumbered them twenty to one. We'll have to give up now, Tom thought and a great pain moved in his chest.

"We still have a field gun on East Haven Green," one of the men was saying. "If we could haul it here—"

"The British will never run from one field-piece," another man said. "Besides, the road to East Haven Green will be swarming with Red-coat guards—and we can't haul a heavy gun through the swamp."

"We have to get it here somehow," Mr. Pardee said. "We can't outfight three thousand Red-coats, but we can make them so uncomfortable that they will wish they were back on their ships."

"And if we don't keep on fighting," another man said, "the Redcoats will raid farther inland and burn more homes and grain fields, and steal more animals to feed their armies."

The men nodded. Tom felt a strange excitement growing in him. These men had been driven from their homes and forced to retreat again and again. There was little chance of their winning a victory but they weren't giving up. They weren't even thinking of giving up.

He wished Elizabeth could hear the men of East Haven now.

"Even if we do slip the fieldpiece past the Redcoat guards," one man was saying, "how can we haul it up the slope far enough to fire on the British at the top?"

"We can take the gun up the old Indian trail," Tom cried. "It's so well hidden, we wouldn't be seen. There's a ledge part way up where we could place a gun. I can show you the way."

"That's it," Mr. Pardee said. "After dark we'll haul that fieldpiece past the Redcoats somehow. Tom, you go up to the ledge and keep watch so we'll be sure the British haven't discovered the trail. We'll signal you from the swamp when we get back with the gun."

The afternoon seemed very long as Tom waited

under the ledge. The night seemed even longer. He could see the bonfires of the Redcoats on the harbor shore below. He heard their shouts as they gathered around the fires and barbecued pigs and chickens and sheep they had caught in the woods. Whenever a breeze brought a whiff of the roasting meat to Tom, he groaned. He was hungry, and angry too.

The roasting pigs and chickens and sheep belonged to his family and their neighbors. The British were roasting them over the very bonfires the Patriots had stacked to celebrate the Fourth of July.

He was glad that Curly-tail was with Elizabeth and his mother. As he thought of his mother, he swallowed a lump in his throat. He hoped she was far enough away to be safe. He hoped his father and John were safe, too. He wouldn't even mind being so hungry if he knew that his family was all right.

It was almost morning when he heard a voice

call softly from the burial ground below. "Tom, we're back."

He slid down the trail and hurried to meet Mr. Pardee with about a hundred men. They had the fieldpiece from East Haven Green with them.

"The trail begins back of this rock and bushes," Tom said excitedly.

He led the way, waiting every few steps for the men who pulled and pushed and strained to haul the big gun along the narrow trail. Twice they had to stop and break off great branches of trees before they could haul the gun past them.

The sun was up by the time the men had the fieldpiece stationed on the ledge. Then the Patriots began to fire on the surprised Redcoats on the hill. The boom of the fieldpiece seemed to be a signal for all the hidden Patriots to fire, too. Muskets sounded from the swamp and from the woods. From every direction Patriot fire raked the British on Beacon Hill.

"Tom," Mr. Pardee called. "We need water to fight in this heat."

Tom caught up the iron kettle from the gun hook and hurried down the trail to the swamp.

Again and again he carried water to the thirsty fighting men and to cool the gun. He thought he must have dragged himself up that trail a hundred times when, toward noon, he handed Mr. Pardee a gourd of water.

"Do you think we will ever drive them away?" Tom asked. "There are so many of them."

Mr. Pardee drank deeply and handed the gourd back to Tom. "I don't know," he said. "They've been carrying plenty of wounded back to their ships."

"Look," Tom cried. "The Redcoats *are* leaving. They're marching almost on a run. They've had enough."

"They do seem to be in a hurry," Mr. Pardee said. His tired, smoke-blackened face broke into a smile. "I guess they didn't expect us to fight so stubbornly against trained soldiers."

As the British left Beacon Hill, the Patriots rushed to man it again. Hundreds of men appeared from the swamps and the woods. They ran up the back of the hill, holding their muskets

before them, and fired on the retreating British. The rear lines of the Redcoats returned the fire but they didn't halt. The exchange of fire continued while the British climbed into their small boats along the shore. Tom watched the Redcoats row to their ships and climb aboard.

"They really mean to leave," he kept saying. It felt funny to be grinning and to feel his eyes blur at the same time.

Even before the enemy ships sailed from the harbor, Tom saw oxcarts and people on foot returning along the cartway below the hill. He shaded his eyes with his hands to see better, but the people were too far away for him to recognize anyone. He could hardly wait for the Patriots to stop firing the fieldpiece so that he would be free to go home.

At last Mr. Pardee said, "We won't need any more water, Tom. We're through fighting."

Tom ran down the Indian trail and reached the cartway. As he hurried toward home, he saw blackened earth on every side, where grain fields had been. All his neighbors' homes were smoldering ruins.

He followed the cartway through the woods. As he came toward the bend in the road which led to his own home, he walked faster and faster. Maybe, just *maybe*, his father's plan had worked. Maybe the British officers had liked the Independence feast left for them and had spared his house.

He turned the bend in the road and stopped. He didn't know whether the British had eaten the feast or not, but nothing remained of the Morris mansion except the stone foundation, the end wall of stone and the chimneys. The cattle barn and stable had burned. Only the new hoghouse, surrounded by bare earth where the hogs rooted, had not caught fire.

Tom stood in the road, and a lump grew and grew in his throat. His beautiful home and all that was in it were gone. Pain moved up in his chest until he was afraid he was going to cry.

Then he saw people near the hoghouse. His

father and John were rounding up stray cows. There was his mother with a food basket on her arm. There were his small sisters and brothers running in the salt grass meadow. And there was Curly-tail following them.

Tom felt so thankful to see them all safe that he blinked and blinked and didn't care if tears rolled down his cheeks.

He heard a crackle of bushes beside the road and saw Elizabeth carrying an armful of quilts. He called to her.

"Tom," she cried as she turned to meet him. "I'm so glad you're safe."

He took some of the quilts from her. "Let me help carry," he said.

"I'm thankful we hid the quilts and dishes and clothes," Elizabeth said. "They're all we have left except the hoghouse. Your father says we'll live in it until he can rebuild the house."

"Live in the hoghouse!" Tom cried.

"It's funny, isn't it?" Elizabeth said. "We were

always telling Curly-tail to keep out of our house. Now we have to live in his."

"You wouldn't think it was so funny if it was your home that was burned," Tom said.

He saw Elizabeth's lip tremble. She felt as bad as he did. She was only trying to make the best of things, like his father and mother, who were making a home of the hoghouse.

"I–I didn't mean that," Tom apologized.

"I know," Elizabeth said. "You must be awfully hungry, Tom. There's food left–we have bread and pudding and roast."

"Then let's hurry and collect the china and dig up the silver," Tom said. "We may have to live in a pig's house but Mother will never let us eat like one."

As they walked along the road, their arms piled chin-high with quilts, Elizabeth said, "Where were you, Tom, during the fighting?"

"I was in it," he said.

He told her how their neighbors had fought

against trained soldiers and had been driven back, and how they fought again and again even when there seemed no chance of victory. He told her of Mr. Tuttle and Josiah, who faced the enemy and chose the dungeon of a prison ship and the loss of their property because they believed in freedom.

"They must have been trembling, with swords at their back," Tom said, "but Mr. Tuttle's voice didn't shake when he spoke. All they asked him to say was that he would quit and never fight the British again."

"But he wouldn't!" she said. "Oh, Tom, no one in Philadelphia was braver than that."

Tom's throat felt so full he couldn't say a word. But he knew he would never be cross with Elizabeth again when she talked of Philadelphia. Now he understood how she felt. He had discovered the wonderful meaning which the words of the Declaration of Independence held for her. Today he had seen his own family and neighbors risk their lives and fortunes for liberty.

"And you were very brave, Tom," Elizabeth said, "to warn Mrs. Tuttle and go back for her papers and help the men at Beacon Hill. Weren't you afraid?"

Tom didn't know how to answer. He shifted the quilts in his arms and sniffed the smell of rain in the sea breeze. Rain would help the burned fields to grow green again.

"I was frightened," Elizabeth admitted, "from the moment we began to hide the valuables."

"I guess I was, too," Tom said at last. "But I found out—even when you're afraid, you can do what you need to do."

FOURTH OF JULY RAID *is fiction based on historical fact. New Haven, Connecticut, had planned its first big celebration of Independence Day in 1779. The Fourth, which fell on Sunday, was to be observed on Monday.*

On July fifth, General Tyron with British troops invaded New Haven. They burned the houses in their march along the harbor shore in the area known as East Haven. (Another division of British troops attacked New Haven proper, where townspeople, Foot Guards and Yale students combined to resist them.)

Recorded in histories of East Haven are the words of Joseph Tuttle when he defied the British before his home, the story of the feast set up by Captain Amos Morris in an effort to save his home, and descriptions of the stand at Beacon Hill.

The beautiful Morris mansion at Solitary Cove was the first building to be set afire. Later Captain Morris wrote the Connecticut General Assembly about his losses and said that his large family was forced to live in the hoghouse until he could rebuild his home.

The Morris house was rebuilt in 1780. It has been preserved for historical interest and visitors are welcome. Worship is still held in the Stone Meeting House (now called Old Stone Church) in East Haven, where some townspeople took refuge during the raid.